Counting Ca

Written by Michi Fujimoto
Based on the teleplay "Good Old George"
by Paul Germain and Joe Ansolabehere

PRICE STERN SLOAN
Los Angeles

Published by Price Stern Sloan, Inc., a member of The Putnam & Grosset Group, New York, New York.

Library of Congress Catalog Card Number: 94-68592
ISBN: 0-8431-3839-4
First Edition
1 3 5 7 9 10 8 6 4 2

What a mess! Muddy paw prints are all over the floor. Bags of food lay torn open. And what's that pink goo in the bathroom? Who could have made such a mess . . . and who's making that loud slurping noise? Beethoven! He's drinking water in the bathroom again. And he's covered in mud!

Beep-beep! A car drives up to the house. George Newton is home from work.

Beethoven rushes to the door to greet him.

"Honey, I'm . . ." George starts to speak but looks around the house and drops his briefcase. "BEETHOVEN!!!" He can't believe how messy the house is.

"You've destroyed my house. You're making me crazy!" George screams. He leads the St. Bernard out the back door.

But Beethoven has rubbed his fur against George, and now George is dirty, too!

Locking Beethoven into his kennel, George yells, "Stay here!"

But Beethoven doesn't mind. He thinks George is just playing around.

Sparky, the neighborhood stray, peeks over the fence to visit his best pal.

"Hey, Beethoven, how's it going?" he asks.

"Pretty good," Beethoven answers. "I think George is starting to like me." He wags his tail as George slams the door.

Later, Alice Newton and the Newton kids—Ryce, Ted, and Emily—watch George pace in the kitchen.

"I hate him, Alice!" George screams.

"You don't hate Beethoven, George," Alice tells her husband.

"Daddy, Beethoven didn't do anything on purpose. He loves you," Emily says.

But George is still convinced that Beethoven is out to get him!

Outside, Beethoven stares at George through the window. “He’s the best master a dog could have,” Beethoven says, sighing. Sparky watches George pace back and forth and wave his hands in the air. Sparky shakes his head. He doesn’t agree with Beethoven.

"Oh, you just don't know him, that's all," Beethoven says. "He takes me for a walk every day, combs my fur, and lets me eat his shoes!" Beethoven searches for something in his kennel. *Clank! Crash!* "Ah-ha!"

Beethoven brings out an old, over-chewed, and over-slobbered ball. It's a doggy masterpiece, and Sparky is impressed. "It's beautiful!" Sparky says.

Beethoven tells Sparky that George gave him the ball.

"See, when I was little I couldn't sleep at night," Beethoven explains. "So George gave me this ball to keep me company. After that I slept like a puppy, and I've been sleeping with it ever since!"

Sparky throws the ball around. Beethoven worries that his ball might get lost or caught in a tree.

But Sparky is having fun! He bounces the ball on his nose and the ball goes higher and higher. Beethoven doesn't like this at all. What if something were to happen to his favorite ball?

Just then, Sparky loses control of the ball, and it goes over the fence!

The ball bounces across the street, where a city worker shoves branches into a tree mulcher. *Buzz*. The branches come out as sawdust. *Buzz*. Beethoven's ball bounces into the tree mulcher and—*Brrff*—the ball comes out as a puff of smoke.

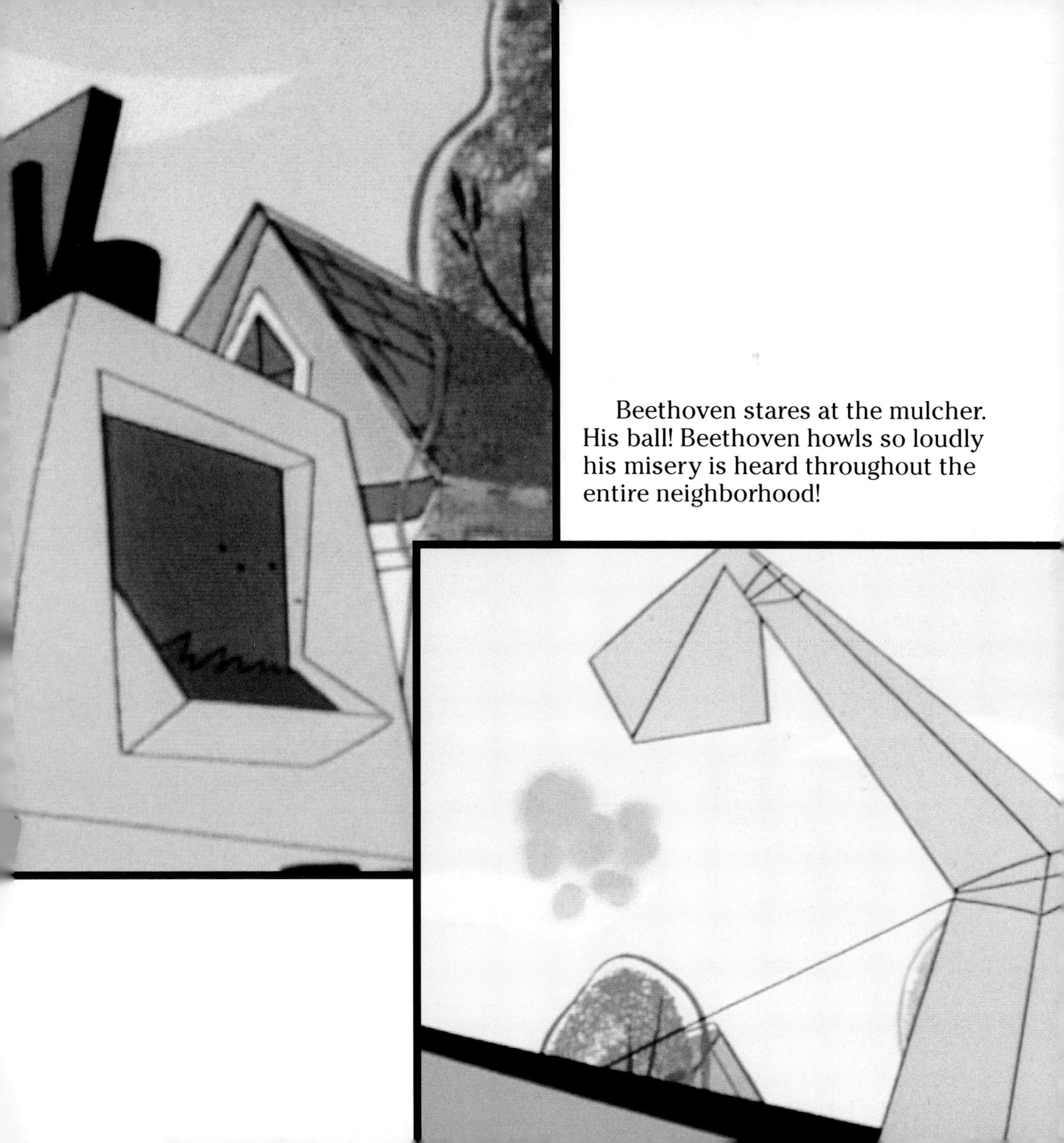

Beethoven stares at the mulcher. His ball! Beethoven howls so loudly his misery is heard throughout the entire neighborhood!

That night, Beethoven tries to fall asleep. He tosses and turns in his doggy bed. *Aaargh!* It's no use!

Beethoven tries counting cats. Closing his eyes, imaginary cats appear. "One . . . two . . . thr— Hey! Hey, you cat, get out of there!" Beethoven hits his blanket.

Counting cats doesn't help. If only he could find something—or someone—to sleep next to. But who? George!

Beethoven pushes the kennel gate open and tippy-paws toward the house. Pushing in the basement window, he jumps in.

Once inside, Beethoven trots up the stairs. I'll sleep next to George, Beethoven thinks. Sure, he's my master.

Beethoven peeks into George and Alice's bedroom and smiles. Good old George! *Creak!* The bed squeaks underneath the St. Bernard's big body as he crawls on. Standing over George, Beethoven lets a string of drool fall out of his mouth . . . and into George's mouth!

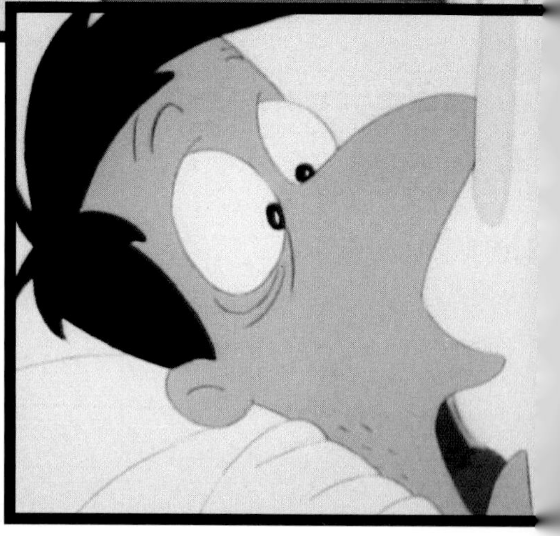

"*Agggghhhh*—Beethoven!" George screams.

Beethoven smiles. That George! In the corner of the kennel, Beethoven pushes aside his dog dish. A secret tunnel is hidden underneath! Beethoven crawls through the tunnel. He's free again!

George shoves Beethoven into his kennel outside. A big chain locks the kennel tight.

"See if you can get out of that!" George says, marching back into the house.

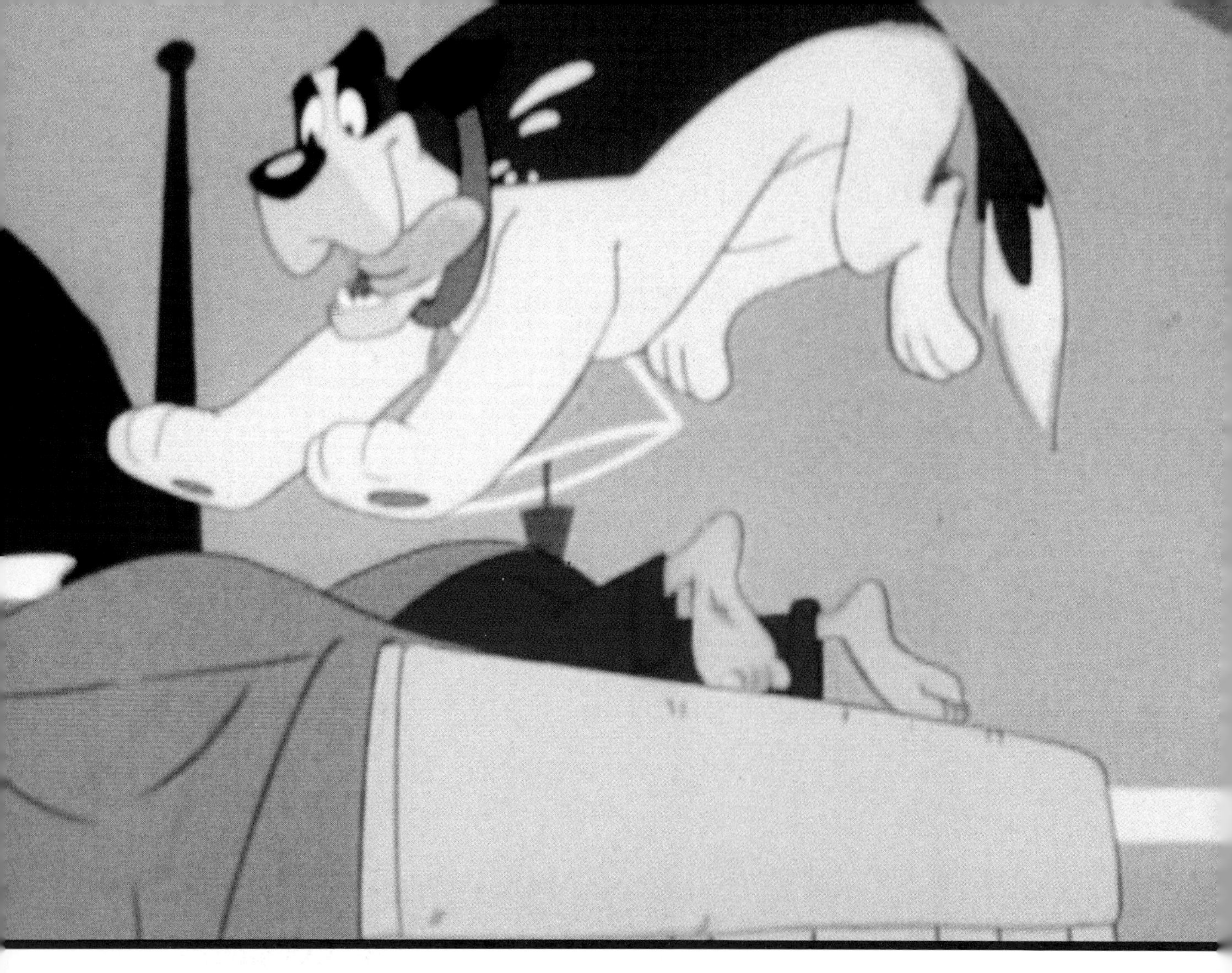

"There's no way that Beethoven can get out now," George tells Alice in their bedroom, yawning. He turns off the light.

Beethoven runs in and jumps into the air. *Ka-bam!* Beethoven lands on the bed, and it crashes to the floor!

"Beethoven!"

Kennel time for Beethoven! But not for long. . . .

Upstairs, Alice watches George place their bed over several paint cans.

“Honey, are you sure putting the bed on paint cans is a good idea?” she asks.

“What could be more stable than two dozen cans of paint?” George responds.

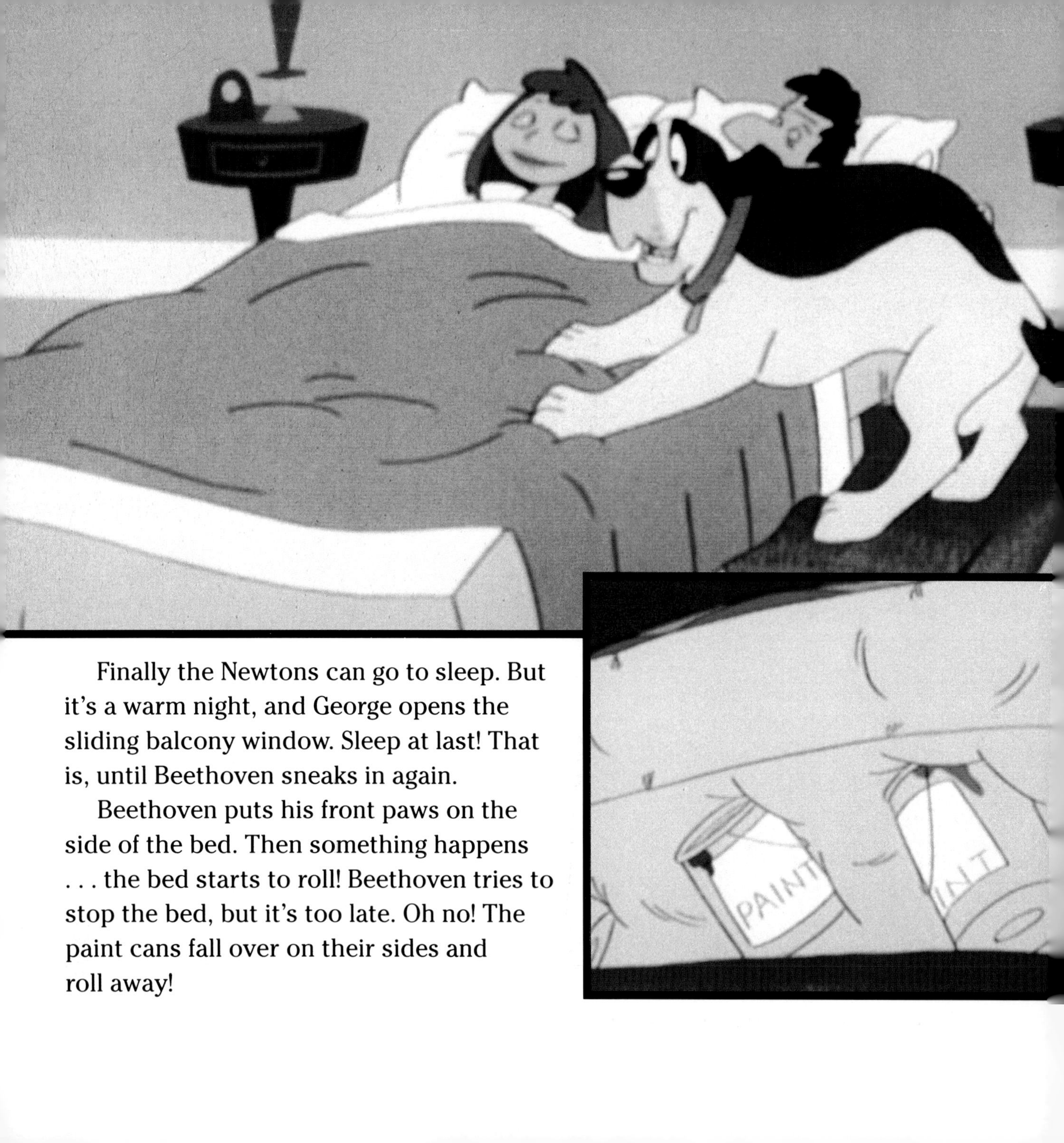

Finally the Newtons can go to sleep. But it's a warm night, and George opens the sliding balcony window. Sleep at last! That is, until Beethoven sneaks in again.

Beethoven puts his front paws on the side of the bed. Then something happens . . . the bed starts to roll! Beethoven tries to stop the bed, but it's too late. Oh no! The paint cans fall over on their sides and roll away!

The bed and the paint cans roll toward the open window.

"*Yaaahhh!*" George and Alice scream.

The bed flies through the window. *Crash!* The bed lands right in the middle of the backyard.

Slowly, paint cans roll off the balcony. One by one. Paint splatters everywhere, including on George and Alice!

"Bee-tho-ven!" George and Alice yell.

Beethoven looks down from the balcony. Oh-oh.

“You’re a menace, Beethoven!” George yells. He hammers a post in the backyard. “You’ve kept me up all night long and destroyed the entire back of my house!” Then George ties one end of a chain to the post. On the other end of the chain is Beethoven.

“And if you try to escape again, I’m giving you away to Mrs. Jergensen,” George threatens. Beethoven’s eyes grow wide. Mrs. Jergensen—the one with all the cats! George must really mean it this time!

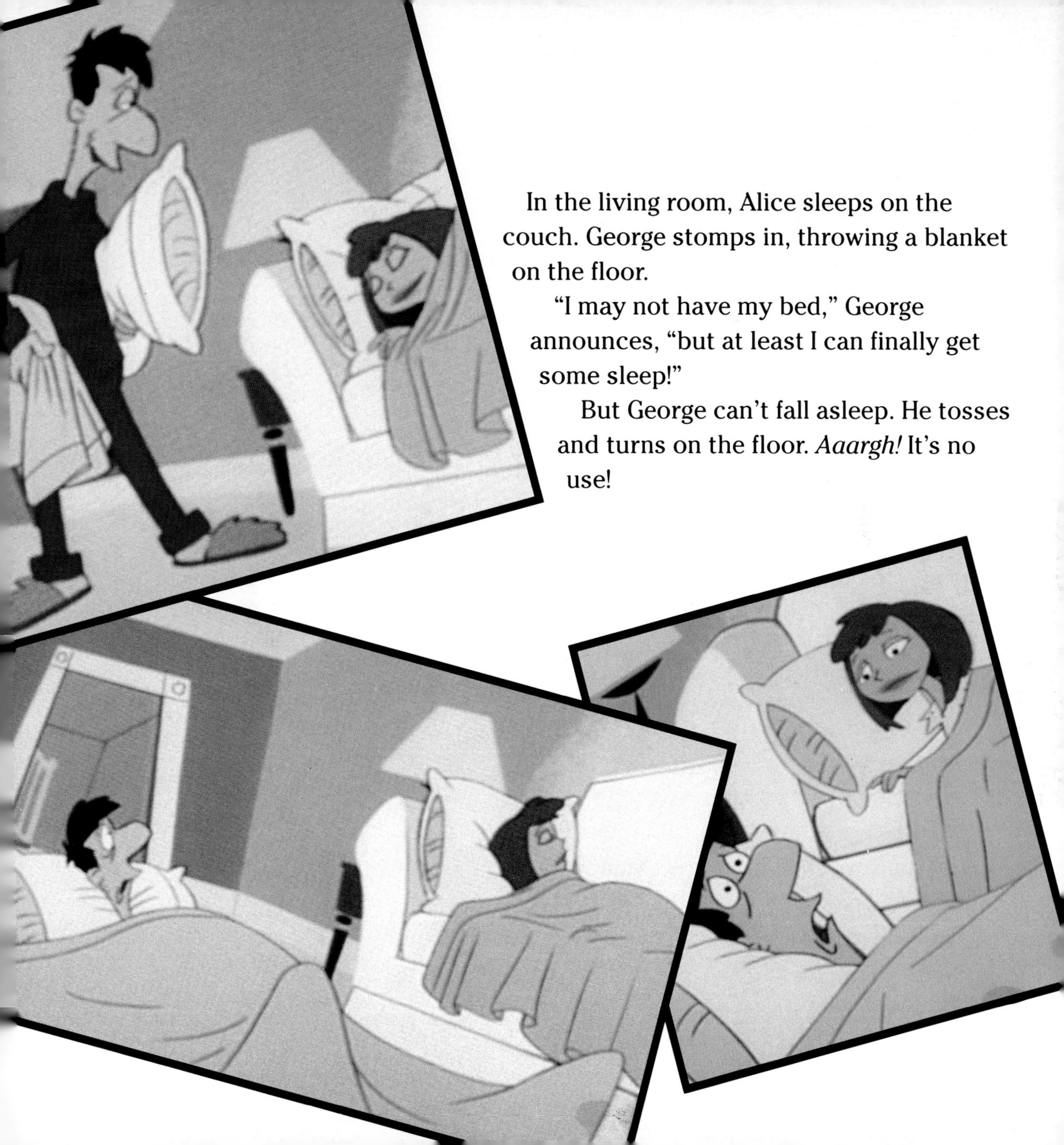

In the living room, Alice sleeps on the couch. George stomps in, throwing a blanket on the floor.

"I may not have my bed," George announces, "but at least I can finally get some sleep!"

But George can't fall asleep. He tosses and turns on the floor. *Aaargh!* It's no use!

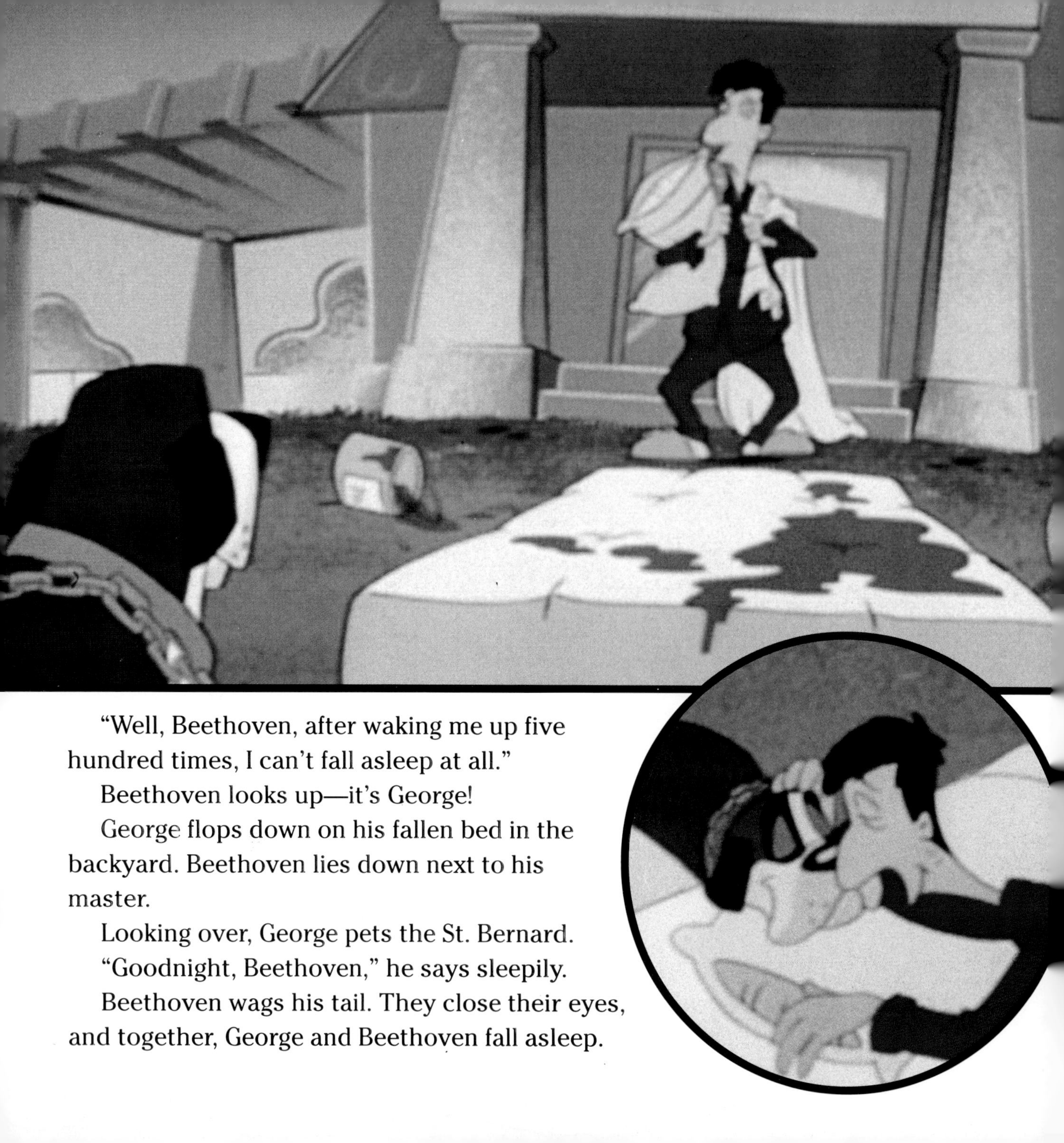

"Well, Beethoven, after waking me up five hundred times, I can't fall asleep at all."

Beethoven looks up—it's George!

George flops down on his fallen bed in the backyard. Beethoven lies down next to his master.

Looking over, George pets the St. Bernard.

"Goodnight, Beethoven," he says sleepily.

Beethoven wags his tail. They close their eyes, and together, George and Beethoven fall asleep.